MW01599774

Ten Steps to Success

HOW TO BUILD A BUSINESS
ONE STEP AT A TIME

....

Denise Walthers

Copyright Direct Selling Leadership Center 2010

INTELLECTUAL PROPERTY NOTICE

This material and these concepts are the intellectual property of
the Direct Selling Leadership Center.

You may not repackage or resell this program without express
written authorization. 2010

ISBN: 978-1-61658-205-0

DIRECT SELLING LEADERSHIP CENTER
Denise Walthers
St. Petersburg, FL

http://www.directsellingleadershipcenter.com

Coaching and Leadership training designed specifically for the direct selling or
multi-level marketing industries

CONTENTS

Acknowledgement

There are so many people who have helped me along the way. I want to
especially thank Vicki Miller for creating the assessment test and for being
my life coach and supporting me to take risks. Thanks also to JoAnne Jaeger,
my mentor and special friend. Deborah Dickson, my editor and collaborator
who helped put my thoughts into words. The customers, team members and
corporate staff who have supported my business along the way are too numerous
to mention, but I embrace and thank them with all my heart.
My husband, William, who has supported me throughout my career and
our children, Jennifer and Jonathan, who are entrepreneral thinkers
and young adults we are both so proud of.

Message from Denise

I have been in direct sales for the past twenty years, both as a Consultant, as well as on the corporate support side of the business. I know in my heart direct sales has empowered me as a woman to be a stronger person, as well as evolve into a savvy businesswoman. What started out as a means to take my family on trips when our children were small blossomed into a career that took me across the United States to both coasts, and everywhere in between. Direct Sales has opened more doors and introduced me to more wonderful people, travel and amazing adventures than I ever imagined possible.

It is my desire to give back to an industry that has done so much for my own life. The Direct Selling Leadership Center was founded as a way to mentor others in the wonderful world of direct sales and to help in supporting people to become all they can be. The Direct Selling Leadership Center is a training ground to show you how to become successful in your personal life and business. It is through great networking organizations like the DSA and the DSWA that women are finding that by helping one another along the way, it helps us all to grow and attain our deepest and most passionate desires.

Let's say yes to opportunity and together find a way to make it happen! We are here for you and are looking forward to taking this wonderful journey together, and have fun along the way!

Yours Truly,

Denise Walthers

Denise Walthers
President, DSLC
Direct Selling Leadership Center

LEADERSHIP SUCCESS PROGRAM

This Leadership Success Program is an assessment tool for measuring growth in ten different areas of leadership development. The concepts in this quiz will be explored in depth in this guidebook. As you answer each question, reflect on your leadership style, find your blind spots and evaluate your strengths and weaknesses. Learn and grow from this experience. This test is for you — and you only. These benchmarks are areas where you can choose to focus and grow into an entrepreneur who is a strong leader.

In the assessment, there are 100 key factors to foster empowered leadership skills grouped into 10 distinct areas:

- Trust/Integrity
- Inspired Vision
- Understanding the Basics of Your Business
- Be an "Energy Generator"
- Communicate Openly
- Have Clear Priorities
- Be a Change Leader
- Be a Role Model
- Value People
- Accept Responsibility

These are hallmark characteristics to becoming a leader. We will explore concepts like not allowing fear to hold you back, overcoming obstacles, reaching your full potential, and taking steps that will put you in a position of power, leadership and authority. We hope you will feel empowered to take these new steps forward and embrace these concepts with an open mind and winning attitude. You will find that by becoming a mentor to others and recruiting new Consultants, you will take a leadership role and your business, your friendships, your earnings and your life, will flourish.

Your business will never grow beyond your personal growth!

HOW TO USE THIS BOOK

You will step through ten chapters of this book. With each chapter, take the quiz and reflect on how you might improve these aspects of your behavior and attitude. At the end of each chapter you will find an exercise. These tools can help you along your path to success. Some of these tips and tricks I have learned along the way help keep me organized and on top of my business. You may want to alter the tools for use in your own personal work strategy.

Best wishes for your success!

STEP I

....

Trust / Integrity

WORK FROM A BASIS OF INTEGRITY AND TRUST

When running your business the most important thing to consider is fostering trust. When you operate from a basis of integrity, especially in difficult situations, your team members and your customers quickly realize you are a person they can count on. If you make a mistake, own up to it immediately, be honest about the situation, and then try to fix the problem. By giving exceptional service and going beyond what others expect, you will position yourself as a leader and someone people can trust, which is a building block for inspiring loyalty and strong relationships. When others confide in you, it is important to keep their confidences. When you disagree with what they say, be assertive, truthful and honest, while using tact and diplomacy.

Business rapidly changes every day. Keep your team informed about changes and decisions and they will feel more secure, confident and empowered. Follow through and honor your commitments. By demonstrating standards of excellence, your team will follow and live up to your example.

"Understanding how our principles govern our decisions is one of the most dynamic concepts in quickening our success"

Now let's take a look at some specific tips to address each of the 10 areas of Trust / Integrity:

- *I always operate from a base of integrity (honesty), even in difficult situations.*
  The key word in this statement is "always." That means that in every action, every word and every conversation, you conduct yourself with honesty and respectful communication – especially when things are difficult. This isn't always easy, but it is critical to developing the respect and following of those on your team.

- *I under promise and over deliver.*
  Never underestimate the value of meeting your commitments. Your team needs to know that they can count on you and what you say, you will do. This can be challenging, especially for over-achievers, but it is critical to your development as a leader.

- *I work for a company that has high standards and integrity.*
  You can always have confidence that the actions from your company will be taken with the utmost concern and priority for honesty and integrity. What you

must remember is that, to your Consultants and their Customers, **you** are the company. It is your standards and actions that are measured in this evaluation.

- *I can be trusted to maintain confidences.*
  This means when a business associate confides in you, the conversation goes no further. Leaders MUST lead by example and rise above all pettiness and back stabbing. Information given to you is confidential and to divulge that information to others is a betrayal.

- *I tell the truth 100% of the time*
  Always operate from a place of honesty and truth. When you don't know the answer it is all right to say, *"Let me think about that and I'll get back to you."* Consult your higher self when faced with difficulties and you will foster trust and respect.

- *I keep my team informed about changes in the business.*
  It is your responsibility to keep your team well informed. Never assume they will read or find the information for themselves. Communication is key in relationships and business. Follow up on a regularly scheduled basis so your team feels connected.

- *I honor my commitments always.*
  When you say you will do something, be sure to follow through. Others are entrusting you to be a leader they can count on. Never make promises you don't intend to keep.

- *I return all phone calls and answer emails the same day.*
  The tenet of our business is customer service. Try to never keep your customers or team members waiting. If you go out of town, inform them about when you will return and place an outgoing message to that effect on your email and phone.

- *I focus on building long-term relationships with my team.*
  The people you work with are part of your wealth and happiness. Try to never burn bridges unless absolutely necessary and give others the benefit of the doubt. Relationships take work and no one is perfect, but we are all trying to do our best. A truly successful leader makes the people around them feel successful.

- *I teach my team to demonstrate excellent standards of professionalism.*
  Practice and teach high standards in manners, dress, and telephone and email etiquette and sound business practices. Impressions make a difference. Professionalism and maturity are hallmarks of success.

By giving exceptional service and going beyond what others expect, you will position yourself as a leader and someone people can trust.

CHECK THE BOXES THAT APPLY TO YOU

Read the following statements and check what you feel are your strengths. The boxes left blank may indicate areas you may need to work on.

- ❑ I always operate from a base of integrity (honesty), even in difficult situations.
- ❑ I under promise and over deliver.
- ❑ I work for a company that has high standards and integrity.
- ❑ I can be trusted to maintain confidences.
- ❑ I tell the truth 100% of the time.
- ❑ I keep my team informed about changes in the business.
- ❑ I honor my commitments always.
- ❑ I return all phone calls and answer emails the same day.
- ❑ I focus on building long-term relationships with my team.
- ❑ I teach my team to demonstrate excellent standards of professionalism.

___ Number of boxes checked (10 max)

SCORES

0-3 Returning phone calls, keeping commitments and communicating with those around you will help take you into a position of leadership. Are you operating from a position of fear and control, or confidence and commitment? Building long-term relationships takes work, but they are well worth it in the end. A helpful suggestion might be to find a mentor or job coach to help you keep on track.

4-7 You have come a long way and it shows. While you generally make good decisions when it comes to interpersonal relationship skills, there is always room for improvement. Try to hold yourself accountable whenever you make promises, keep confidences or communicate with your team. Honesty goes a long way and you will soon find direct and diplomatic tact is the best way to overcome obstacles and turn problems into opportunities.

8 AND ABOVE You demonstrate the traits of honesty, integrity and clear communication that it takes to be a leader. You engender trust in your relationships, and that's half the battle. People can count on you to be truthful and responsible, and you have the ability to instill confidence in others as a person of your word. You are a true leader!

TRUST/INTEGRITY EXERCISE: A tool to help you deliver your promises and keep up with all you do is a calendar. Create a routine for conducting phone calls, setting appointments, completing your bookkeeping and even doing your household chores. Here is a sample calendar. Design yours to fit your lifestyle.

MONDAY	TUESDAY	WEDNESDAY	THURSDAY	FRIDAY
9-11 A.M. Check email, make phone calls, prepare for week	**9-11 A.M.** Set up appointments for next week	**9-11 A.M.** Send thank you notes and order product	**9-11 A.M.**	**9-11 A.M.** Manage your Web site, check balances review business transactions
11-12 A.M. Confirm appointments for the upcoming week	**11-12 A.M.**	**11-12 A.M.** Touch base with your downline	**11-12 A.M.** Call everyone on your team to make sure they are on track	**11-12 A.M.** Follow up with party attendees
12-1 P.M. Take time out for lunch	**12-1 P.M.** Lunch appointment with potential recruit	**12-1 P.M.** Conduct a one on one with a team leader	**12-1 P.M.** Have lunch with your top producer	**12-1 P.M.** Free time!
1-2 P.M. Bookkeeping and correspondence	**1-2 P.M.**	**1-2 P.M.** Fill out paperwork from the party	**1-2 P.M.**	**1-2 P.M.**
2-3 P.M. Personal housekeeping	**2-3 P.M.**	**2-3 P.M.** Organize bills and correspondence	**2-3 P.M.** Grocery shopping and personal errands	**2-3 P.M.** Write goals for upcoming week
6 P.M.	**6 P.M.** Host a party	**6 P.M.**	**6 P.M.** Host a party	**6 P.M.** Go out with your husband or friends!

- **PINK** - Highlight Recruiting Time with a pink highlighter pen. (This represents new blood, essential to your growth).
- **GREEN** - Highlight selling, parties and one-on-one coaching for consultants with a green highlighter pen. (Represents money)
- **YELLOW** – Highlight in yellow family and personal time (for sunshine!)

STEP 2

Inspired Vision

You were inspired to start your own business for a reason. Everyone's reason may be different. You may love to sell, enjoy meeting new people or have a passion for the product. You might be a businesswoman drawn by the ability to earn a great income with a generous compensation package, or desire an outlet for your creative passions. Whatever your reason, you carry your own vision of what you see for your business.

Great leaders have great minds. The vision you create is what your business can become. You create your own desires, dreams and goals—and you are the driving force behind your vision and theirs too! The goals you can achieve with a clear and concise vision are really limitless. Be willing to ask yourself, "What do I really want?" When you begin to see the possibilities, doors will begin to open up for you.

As you invite others to join your business and communicate the opportunity to them, they will come together as a team to share and help you attain the vision you have for your business. The fears and obstacles in your way can be overcome with positive thoughts, words and actions. By staying focused on your goals and clearly communicating to your team, you will be an inspiration to others, and the rewards you receive will be enormous.

Create a 15 second commercial about your business. Practice saying your commercial aloud. When people ask, "What do you do for a living?" you can reply in a clear, concise way. "I offer a way to improve people's lives with my business," may be one example. Your passion and creativity will blossom with inspired vision for your future and your business.

"The most important goals we can establish are those that will last an eternity."

Now, let's explore each statement and think about how it pertains to you.

- *I have a clear vision of where I am taking my business and what it feels like to be living this vision.*
  Do you know what you want out of your business and can you visualize the future? Picture yourself in your mind's eye making phone calls, approaching acquaintances, selling products and offering personal customer service.
  To clarify your vision, engage in activities like writing a WHY statement.

- *I have communicated my vision to my team.*
  The people who support me have a clear knowledge of what this vision is for my business and their part in it. I have taken time to communicate my intentions and dreams to my family and friends as well as my business associates and team members. To be effective, schedule weekly meetings and phone calls to keep everyone informed about your vision and to keep them on track. Tell a story about how you or someone else achieved their dreams to support your dream in reaching their goals. When they reach their goals, your reach your goals.

- *I replace negative beliefs, attitudes or fears that block my vision with positive thoughts, words and actions.*
  Banish fear and doubt and replace with vitality and enthusiasm. Your thoughts will lead you to your destination. Thinking positively will create positive results.

- *I know my core values and can easily relate these values to my vision.*
  Your beliefs and integrity will guide you. The best business people trust their core instincts, and are guided by their strong values, living by an unwavering commitment to their vision.

- *I continually develop skills or acquire knowledge to support reaching my vision.*
  Ninety percent of success is preparation. Research, learn and hone new skills all the time. Truly successful leaders continually strive to improve themselves. If necessary, take classes at the local continuing education center; find a mentor to help you learn new skills and read, read, read. We gather information in three ways — talking to other people, reading books or watching and listening to tapes or DVDs. The Internet is also a great resource for finding information.

- *I know why I am in this business and can clearly articulate it in one sentence.*
  Practice your 15-second commercial. Refine it if necessary. This is the easiest way to share your vision with others, as word of mouth is always the best advertising. One example might be: *"I'm in this business to touch lives in a positive way through life-changing products."*

- *I understand that I must be accepted as a leader first before my team can buy into my vision.*
  Your team must trust in your abilities and commitment. When they believe in you, they believe in your vision and want to be part of the success.

- *As a visionary leader I help my team move beyond a focus on minor satisfactions to a quest for self-fulfillment.*
  You don't want people who are simply busy, but are led by a goal for their future. Deep fulfillment will come through commitment and personal growth. The best leaders make those around them feel successful. Find and foster each individual's strengths and your team will move forward in extraordinary ways.

- *I know the dreams and visions of my team and seek to help them get what they want.*
  Put yourself in the shoes of your team members. A great leader feels empathy and is able to see the world from the other people's point of view. When you truly know what motivates each individual, you can accomplish great things. Remember, **EMA** is the key to success, everyone wants **EMA** — **E**ncourage, **M**otivate and **A**ppreciate.

- *I hold periodic brainstorming sessions with an innovative core group to spark new ideas or approaches for achieving our visions.*
  Your team members are great resources for new ideas. Take time to ask questions and listen to what they have to say — they can offer a wealth of information when you open yourself up to receive new thoughts and ideas.

CHECK THE BOXES THAT APPLY TO YOU

Read the following statements and check what you feel are your strengths. The boxes left blank may indicate areas you may need to work on.

- ❑ I have a clear vision of where I am taking my business and what it feels like to believing this vision.
- ❑ I have communicated my vision to my team.
- ❑ I replace negative beliefs, attitudes or fears that block my vision with positive thoughts, words and actions.
- ❑ I know my core values and can easily relate these values to my vision.
- ❑ I continually develop skills or acquire knowledge to support reaching my vision.
- ❑ I know why I am in this business and can clearly articulate it in one sentence.
- ❑ I understand that I must be accepted as a leader first, before my team can buy-in to my vision.
- ❑ As a visionary leader I help my team move beyond a focus on minor satisfactions to a quest for self-fulfillment.

❑ I know the dreams and visions of my team and seek to help them get what they want.

❑ I hold periodic brainstorming sessions with an innovative core group to spark new ideas or approaches for achieving our visions.

___ Number of boxes checked (10 max)

SCORES

0-3 You may have the desire — now formulate a clear vision of exactly how you see your business. Talk to others who are successful and write down some of your goals and dreams. This may help you gain clarity of purpose. Women are usually clear about what others want; now stop and ask yourself, "What do *I* want?" When you begin to formulate a clear vision and relate that vision to others, you will find yourself emerging as a leader with a vision.

4-7 You are committed to your business and have a good idea of where you are going. By raising your standards and communicating your vision clearly, you begin to take the next step from being satisfied with your income and lifestyle to being truly fulfilled. When you are confident and enthusiastic and can work with your team toward a common goal, your team will begin looking toward you as a true leader.

8 AND ABOVE You demonstrate the traits of inspiration and vision and have learned the powers of communication it takes to be a leader. People look to you as a person with creative ideas, along with the focus and vision that can help others get what they want as well. You inspire those around you to achieve their goals and in turn you are able to flourish and attain all that you want. With an inspired vision, you *can* have it all!

INSPIRED VISION EXERCISE: When I first started out as a Consultant, I created a dream board. To this day, I have kept my dream board and refer to it to remind me what my original goals and dreams were. To create your dream board, all you need is a poster board, some colored pencils, and a ruler. This exercise will help you clarify your vision and your "why" so you can stay focused on your goals. Guess what – everything I placed on my original dream board and every dream board since has come true!

DREAM BOARD

5 THINGS I WANT TO ACCOMPLISH IN MY LIFE	4 THINGS I VALUE MOST	3 CHALLENGES I FACE	2 OF MY GREATEST ACCOMPLISHMENTS

Write down your answers, then draw a picture or use magazines and glue the pictures to your poster board.

DISCOVER YOUR DREAMS
MY "WHY" IS ...

_____
_____
_____
_____
_____
_____
_____
_____
_____

IF YOU HAD AN UNLIMITED AMOUNT OF MONEY AND TIME:

What are three things you would do?

1. _____
_____

2. _____
_____

3. _____
_____

Where would you go?

_____
_____
_____

What two things would you purchase?

1. _____
2. _____

What are three things you want your Dreams to do for your family, friends and yourself?

1. _____
_____

2. _____
_____

3. _____
_____

STEP 3

$$\cdots\cdots\cdots\cdots\cdots\cdots$$

Understand the Basics of Your Business

Congratulations! You are a new business owner. Being your own boss and in charge of growing your company is one of the best opportunities for financial freedom and personal fulfillment there is. You will discover new ways of doing things, strategies for being disciplined, how to best structure your time and how to network with others to grow your business. This can often feel scary at times, but is also an exciting and enlightening time filled with creativity, learning and action.

There are certain business basics you will need to get started. This is a time to become task oriented and jump in with both feet. Structuring your business and building a solid foundation in the beginning will pay off in the future. These are the building blocks to your future success and must be laid with care and preparation.

"Nearly all men can stand adversity, but if you want to test a man's character, give him power." Abraham Lincoln

Let's talk about each one of the building blocks that are the basics of your business and the steps to your success.

- *I understand that contact is an essential element in leadership.*
  Networking cannot be emphasized enough. In today's changing technological marketplace, communicating your message is more important than ever. Email, cell phone, Internet, and face-to-face contact are all great ways to stay in touch. More than ever before, there is more competition for your face time than ever before. In the words of Suzy Orman "People first, money second, things last." Know that your relationships are the foundation of your business and stay connected with your team. Make a **FRANK** list. A **FRANK** list is an easy way to remember all the people in your life: **F**riends, **R**elatives, **A**cquaintances, **N**eighbors and **K**id's contacts.

- *I challenge team members and hold them accountable for their commitments.*
  It's not enough to ask someone to do something — it is also up to you to make sure it gets done. How many people blame the kids for their house not being in order? Ultimately *you* are the responsible party. Follow through with your commitments and make sure the ones who surround you do so as well.

- *I celebrate the successes of each team member no matter how small.*
  Success is built on a series of small accomplishments. As a leader it is important to recognize others and let them know how important they are.

- *I personally recognize team members' accomplishments at meetings, by email, mail or phone.*
  Gratification and positive rewards really do work. Small gifts, a note or email and a pat on the back go a long way to bringing out the best in others.

- *I understand the desires of my team and how to best motivate them.*
  Everyone is motivated by different "pay offs." Some want more money, some are driven by freedom over their time, and others enjoy socializing and meeting people. Tapping into what motivates your team members individually is a key to inspiring them to be all they can be.

- *I replicate what I am doing by training new sales managers in my team.*
  Duplication of initiatives is key to growing your business. The best business leaders mentor others and train them how to do what they do. When you find people who have the desire and are teachable it is your job to show them the way. Enlisting the help of others is like multiplying your own efforts.

- *I understand part of my leadership role is to coach others to take responsibility.*
  Doing for others is not nearly as important as teaching others to do for themselves. By holding your team members accountable and letting them be responsible for their actions, you are supporting their growth and success. "Never walk alone." When you're doing a party bring a new Consultant with you.

- *I resist the urge to tell others what to do and instead, use open-ended questions to guide them to their own solutions.*
  Rather than asking a yes/no question, show a real interest in your team members by asking questions that elicit a thoughtful response. Remember, this is about them and their goals and dreams. You can guide and support while allowing them to reach their own conclusions. Encourage others to take the lead.

- *I have identified the high-performing 20% of my team so that I can train and encourage them with weekly contact.*
  In sales, 20% of the people do the majority of the work. But invariably, we tend to spend our time with the 80% of low-performers on our team. Try not to fall into this trap. Spend your energy on the cream of the crop to yield higher results.

- *I **CARE** enough about each team member to let them know through: **C**ommunication, **A**ppreciation, **R**ecognition, and **E**ncouragement.*

CHECK THE BOXES THAT APPLY TO YOU

Read the following statements and check what you feel are your strengths.
The boxes left blank may indicate areas you may need to work on.

- ❑ You can never show enough how much you care.
- ❑ I understand that contact is an essential element in leadership.
- ❑ I challenge team members and hold them accountable for their commitments.
- ❑ I celebrate the successes of each team member no matter how small.
- ❑ I personally recognize team members' accomplishments at meetings, by email, mail or phone.
- ❑ I understand the desires of my team and how to best motivate them.
- ❑ I replicate what I am doing by training new sales managers in my team.
- ❑ I understand part of my leadership role is to coach others to take responsibility.
- ❑ I resist the urge to tell others what to do and instead, use open-ended questions to guide them to their own solutions.
- ❑ I have identified the high-performing 20% of my team so that I can coach and encourage them with weekly contact.
- ❑ I **CARE** enough about each team member to let them know through: Communication, Appreciation, Recognition, and Encouragement.

___ Number of boxes checked (10 max)

SCORES

0-3 Building a team requires building up people. If you feel your interpersonal relationship skills need some work, it is often helpful to find a mentor or job coach to help you. Communication is a learned skill and one that can be fostered. Try reading *How to Get What you Want* by John Gray. Join networking groups like the ewomen network (www.ewomen.com) of local business chapters in your area. Practice new communication approaches with your friends and family members and you will soon see others responding to your newfound sense of reaching out to others.

4-7 You have shown you are a caring person willing to support and help others grow. Keep realizing that showing small signs of recognition and treating others with respect and integrity will help you become a better leader. Honor those around you and always treat others, as you would have them treat you.

8 AND ABOVE   You show signs of advanced communication and leadership skills. Those around you look toward you for inspiration and support. They can count on you to hold them to high standards of performance and know you will be right there with them every step of the way.

UNDERSTAND THE BASICS OF YOUR BUSINESS EXERCISE:

Networking is the key to having a successful business. There are tools either on your computer on on-line to help you keep up with your contacts. It is important to jot down a list of everyone in your life you may know.

Friends Old friends from high school, work, clubs.
Relatives including in-laws!
Acquaintances professionals you use like dentists and CPAs, teachers, people from church.
Neighbors meet the people in your area!
Kid's contacts their friends parents, teachers, coaches, etc.

MY FRANK LIST

FRIENDS	RELATIVES	ACQUAINTANCES	NEIGHBORS	KIDS CONTACTS

STEP 4

Be an
Energy Generator

The laws of attraction are always at work. If you are positive, energetic, passionate and motivated, that is the kind of people you will attract to your business and your life. Like attracts like and you will find that many people on your team will have similarities. When you dress for success, instill the practices of being a good leader, maintain a positive attitude and run your business professionally, you will attract the same.

How do you keep a positive attitude and a high level of energy? By taking responsibility for your actions, by living without regret, gossip or other energy-depleting sources, and by loving what you do and finding the joy in it. When you experience day-to-day joy in your business, that is infectious and others take notice. You can't help but foster an environment of success with all the good energy you send out.

"All our dreams can come true, if we have the courage to pursue them." Walt Disney

- *I love what I do and it shows.*
  Do you lie in bed before you go to sleep at night contemplating tomorrow's activities? Do you wake up looking forward to projects and people you will meet? Are you excited that you are the master of your time and run your own business? Your attitude about your life and business shows, and people will take notice. If you find joy in what you do, others will wonder what you're up to and will want to learn from you.

- *I am passionate about my business, my team and serving others.*
  When you tell others about your business and recite your 15-second commercial followed up with your "I" Story, do you have passion in your voice? Whether in person or on the telephone, people can hear this. You are selling a valuable service and product that will help others. If you are excited about helping people meet their needs, they will be receptive to what you have to give. Being of service to others is an ideal that serves all of us well.

- *I make a conscious choice to be positive about my business and to reflect such.*
  Your thoughts and beliefs will lead your actions. Do you feel positive about your business? Have you made a conscious decision to share your business and be the best leader you can be? Your attitude shows to everyone you come in contact with, and is controlled by what you think about. So think great thoughts and great things will happen!

- *I know what restores my energy and I schedule time for such activities each week.*
  Health is manifested mentally and physically. Take good care of yourself through nutrition, exercise and a balanced lifestyle. Take time to sit still each day and listen to your thoughts to plan your strategies for success. Staying too busy often creates a chaotic lifestyle. Take time for yourself each day to practice restorative activities like walking, meditation, and relaxation. You can only take care of others if your own needs are met.

- *I start each morning enthusiastic about what's ahead.*
  Are you excited about picking up the phone and talking with your team members? Do you look forward to having coffee with a neighbor who said she would love to Host a Party? It takes just as much energy to have a good attitude as a bad one, but a good one will accomplish much more and generate more energy and fun! Read *The Power of Positive Thinking* by Norman Vincent Peale or *The Greatest Salesman in the World* by Og Mandino.

- *I know that my attitude, as a leader, is picked up more quickly by my team than my actions.*
  A good attitude goes a long way. When you have a positive attitude, obstacles seem manageable. People pick up on clues though your voice, body language and facial expressions that you accept them in a positive light. You can be the hardest worker in the world, but if you have a negative attitude, your actions are negated.

- *I quickly deal with anything that depletes my energy (i.e. clutter, unanswered mail, piles of papers or forms, broken equipment, etc.)*
  Unfinished projects or broken equipment, whether you are aware of it or not, depletes your energy. When you walk through a house that has piles of laundry or dishes in the sink, your subconscious is thinking, "I need to take care of that." This zaps your subconscious, limiting its freedom to think of stimulating ideas. If you feel the need to hire a maid or lawn boy to take care of some of your chores, then do so. This will free you up to dedicate your energy to what you're really good at—running your business so you can afford to pay for work you don't really enjoy. If you can think of some simple daily systems to take care of your correspondence, phone calls and book keeping, these won't pile up to be a big project that depletes your energy.

- *My team is motivated, productive, and excited about their success.*
  When people feel they have boundless energy and are free of self-imposed limitations, they are motivated and enthusiastic—and can accomplish great

things. Many of our obstacles in life are self-imposed. It is amazing what we can accomplish when we get out of our own way.

- *I know that it's not circumstances that affect my energy, that instead, it is my reaction to these circumstances.*
  Problems and situations, if approached the right way, can in fact be an opportunity to succeed. Circumstances are life's way of challenging you to tackle new situations. It's how you approach problems that will affect their outcome.

- *If problems arise within the team, I address them immediately rather than put them off.*
  Never allow fear or procrastination to enter into it. When there are issues that need to be addressed, don't wait for them to fester, but try to diffuse the situation with the directness and honesty befitting a leader. Try not to be *reactive,* but as unemotional as possible, assess the situation and arrive at a solution that works best for all parties involved. The best negotiators use humor, a great attitude and honesty to address problems.

CHECK THE BOXES THAT APPLY TO YOU

Read the following statements and check what you feel are your strengths.
The boxes left blank may indicate areas you may need to work on.

- ❑ I love what I do and it shows.
- ❑ I am passionate about my business, my team and serving others.
- ❑ I make a conscious choice to be positive about my business and to reflect such.
- ❑ I know what restores my energy, and I schedule time for such activities each week.
- ❑ I start each morning enthusiastic about what's ahead.
- ❑ I know that my attitude, as a leader, is picked up more quickly by my team than my actions.
- ❑ I quickly deal with anything that depletes my energy (i.e. – clutter, unanswered mail, piles of papers or forms, broken equipment, etc).
- ❑ My team is motivated, productive, and excited about their success.
- ❑ I know that it's not circumstances that affect my energy, that instead, it is my reaction to these circumstances.
- ❑ If problems arise within the team, I address them immediately rather than put it off.

___ Number of boxes checked (10 max)

SCORES

0-3 In the words of Ralph Waldo Emerson, "Don't be too timid and squeamish about your actions. All life is an experiment. The more experiments you make the better." As a leader, you are a person who is willing to act. You make decisions quickly by consulting your instincts and have the confidence to try new things. Remember that your attitude is controlled by your thoughts, so try thinking positive thoughts and great things will begin to happen. Rid your world of clutter and crazy makers so you will be freed up to be the best you can be!

4-7 You are well on you way to being an Energy Generator but could make steps to add more balance in your life. What depletes your energy? What do you worry about the most? Money, marriage, unfinished business? Try to stop worrying and see what happens. When you begin to replace those old thoughts of worry and sadness with new thoughts of joy and happiness, your energy will begin to change! Your newfound attitude will affect all areas of your life, and those around you will notice. When you are pain free and worry free, things will begin to untangle and free you up to generate all kinds of good things around you.

8 AND ABOVE You are clearly an energy generator! You love what you do and have attracted others to share in your passion! You have made the conscious choice to be positive about your business and it shows. You take time out of every day to recharge and restore your energy and wake up each morning excited to start the day! Your attitude allows you to banish negative emotions, clutter and unanswered mail, and your team is producing and generating wealth and happiness. You react to problems as challenges, approaching them as a game you are sure to win! Encourage them to keep moving as we have at the previous levels – even if they are at the top – "Keep on generating … it's contagious!"

BE AN ENERGY GENERATOR EXERCISE: Booking shows is one way I keep the energy going. Here is a list of what I do to keep a positive mental attitude and generate energy. Booking shows is the key to your business success. The more shows you book and hold, the stronger your business will become.

FIRST: Complete your FRANK List and call or talk with every person on it.	Set a goal to talk with 5 new people every day.	Hit the Streets! Go to malls, parks, restaurants, etc., and pass out your business cards … Don't forget to get phone numbers in exchange!	Give a catalog with your business card to every person who serves you at a grocery store, hair salon, dry cleaners, doctors office, etc.
Make Customer Calls – Contact past customers about re-ordering and new catalogs (the conversation could lead to a show). Don't forget to ask for referrals.	Talk to the teachers at a local day care or school. Have catalogs and business cards available.	Place an inexpensive classified ad in local publications targeted to women, parents, as well as in your neighborhood newsletter.	Wear your name tag and introduce yourself at the next Chamber of Commerce meeting in your community.
	Join a networking group.	Invite a potential recruit or hostess to lunch.	Join a social networking website.
Listen to the conference calls. Stay up with latest company promotions.	Send your spouse to work with catalogs. What is your husband willing to do to help you make a six figure income?	Call customers who placed an outside order and invite them to host a show.	Post a flyer on every bulletin board you see.

WHAT'S YOUR 30-SECOND COMMERCIAL?

Example: "Hi, I'm _____. I am so fortunate to have a career with financial freedom and flexibility. I sell a product people love. Are you interested in hearing about what I do?"

Find your local festival and hand out your brochures at a booth. Share and demonstrate your product.	Host a party. Invite 10 friends to come.	When you host a party, let the guests know you will give them a gift for referring Bookings.
Wear your name tag. People will ask about your business.	Sign up for inexpensive local vendor events.	Visit local businesses and suggest gifts for employees and clients. Especially around the holidays! Post a flyer on every bulletin board you see.
Offer to do an Demonstration at your local Church for Women's Events.	Let your neighbors know about your business - be sure each one has a current catalog. Host a neighborhood party.	Ask for (and give a gift for) referrals. "Who do you know who might be interested in hosting a party or a new career?"
	Use as gifts for teachers, postal workers, hairdressers, coaches, etc.	

STEP 5

. . . .

Communicate Openly

Direct sales involves talking with people — lots of people. There are some effective ways — and not so effective ways — which we have learned to communicate with others. Good communication is a skill that can constantly be improved. There are numerous books on the subject that can be helpful for honing your skills. How you communicate is as individual as you are. Effective communication involves the giving and receiving of information and oftentimes can be persuasive and elicit a change in behavior or attitude.

"Give whatever you are doing and whoever you are with the gift of your attention." Jim Rohn

- *I have regularly scheduled times to communicate with my team.*
  The Webster's Dictionary defines a habit as a continual, often involuntary or unconscious inclination to perform an activity, acquired through frequent repetition. When you get in the *habit* of communicating with your team on a regular basis, you will automatically increase your communication. To learn more about putting good habits to work in your life, read Stephen Covey's *7 Habits of Highly Effective People*. This book is one of the best self-help books ever written to help you shift into taking initiative to use good habits to improve your life and your relationships. Set a goal to call your main team leaders once a week and mark specific times on your calendar. Remember the 80/20 rule and give your time and energy to the 20% who are doing most of the work and activity. Also set scheduled times to contact potential recruits, new recruits and Hostesses. Don't wait for others to contact you — pick up the phone and make the call.

- *I understand everyone has a different style of communication and I look for clues on how to communicate with people on an individual basis.*
  If you learn how to read body language and listen closely to others, you will master how to communicate with them in a way they can understand. For instance, some people are more casual, others more formal. If you are able to use intuition to tap into their personality style, your can better communicate with them.

- *I use a supportive communication style, seeking to make team members feel good about themselves.*
  Are there some people you feel more likely to confide in than others? What makes some people easier to talk to and engage in conversation? Usually those who make a concerted effort to listen and not pre-judge are more likely to

become a trusted confidant. Some people have that special gift of being able to make others feel good about themselves. Calling people by their names, remembering details about their likes and dislikes, having a capacity for empathy are traits of a good listener, which makes a good communicator. Reflect on how you can build esteem and trust with members of your team. Try to encourage better communication through offering supportive words of encouragement.

- *I continually seek new ways to improve my communication skills.*
  There are many helpful books on the subject. Some of my personal favorites are *How to Talk so People Listen* by Sonya Hamlin, *Getting Past No* by Jim Camp and the classic, *How to Win Friends and Influence People* by Dale Carnegie. All these books teach strategies for negotiating more effectively, the art of persuasion to use communication to change behavior.

- *I frequently interact with team members at all levels.*
  Get in front of your people! Ask a new recruit for coffee, invite your team to lunch or even set up a conference call. Nowadays there are so many ways to communicate! Most of all have fun and enjoy interacting with your team members. The more you can make time to talk with your team, the more quickly you build the relationships that will grow your business.

- *I practice effective listening, giving others opportunity to share their input.*
  Sometimes the most important part of communicating is knowing when not to talk and listen to the other person. Actively listening is really understanding and hearing what she has to say — not formulating your response or waiting for her to finish so you can speak. Effective listening is active and shows empathy and understanding. Paraphrasing is a good method of feedback to make sure you heard someone correctly. Also be aware of your body language such as looking the speaker in the eye, nodding your head in approval and holding your body in a non-defensive open stance that encourages information. Be sure to ask questions to prompt the speaker. You can learn how to gather valuable information when you take the time to listen to what others have to say.

- *I am truthful and consistent in my communications, sharing the information with each person.*
  Your team members will know when you play favorites. Communicate information directly and openly with all members of your team. If someone tells you something in confidence — keep it confidential. Otherwise, information that applies to the group should be communicated with everyone on your team. Emails are a great way to disseminate information.

- *I deliver unpleasant news in person, when possible, and in a calm, non-judgmental manner.*

  This means lose the drama! Deliver news that is difficult face to face and with compassion, in a calm and professional manner. Avoid being critical or judgmental with comments or body language, as this will put the person on the receiving end on defense immediately. Situations and problems are bound to occur but, when handled in a mature, rational manner can become an opportunity for growth and knowledge. Conflicts and ill feelings can often be resolved through open communication and understanding.

- *I understand that the purpose of communication is not just to convey information but also to change behavior by persuading people to take action.*

  Effective communication can be a powerful persuasive device. People are motivated strongly by two things: fear and reward. When you are a leader, you are dealing with people's lives and income. Therefore, you have a huge responsibility to treat others with fairness and honesty. When you can inspire them and persuade them to alter their behavior in ways that will benefit them, you are an effective communicator and leader. When you know what their "why" is and what motivates them, you can tap into their passions and energy. People have an incredible amount of energy when their goals are clear and they know you believe in them.

- *I listen to learn, to grow, to encourage and to convey that I care.*

  We are here to learn from one another. When you are open to receive knowledge from others, you are placing yourself in a position of learning and growth. With a positive attitude and caring heart, there's nothing you can't accomplish!

CHECK THE BOXES THAT APPLY TO YOU

Read the following statements and check what you feel are your strengths. The boxes left blank may indicate areas you may need to work on.

- ❑ I have regularly scheduled times to communicate with my team.
- ❑ I understand everyone has a different style of communication and I look for clues to on how to communicate with people on an individual basis.
- ❑ I use a supportive communication style, seeking to make team members feel good about them.

❑ I continually seek new ways to improve my communication skills.

❑ I frequently interact with team members at all levels.

❑ I practice effective listening, giving others opportunity to share their input.

❑ I am truthful and consistent in my communications, sharing the information with each person.

❑ I deliver unpleasant news in person, when possible, and in a calm, non-judgmental manner.

❑ I understand that the purpose of communication is not just to convey information but also to change behavior by persuading people to take action.

❑ I listen to learn, to grow, to encourage and to convey that I care.

___ Number of boxes checked (10 max)

SCORES

0-3 Try to determine what is holding you back from communicating more effectively. Shyness, fear of rejection or failure, or lack of knowledge or confidence may contribute to your lack of quality communication. There are many networking groups like Toastmasters, International Association of Business Communicators, women in business organizations and others that can help you practice this skill. Communication is largely a learned behavior, and poor communication can be unlearned and improved upon.

4-7 You are a good, solid communicator but could improve through reading helpful books or practicing your communication skills on others. Are you an active listener? Ask someone close to you how you may improve your communication skills. Make a conscious effort to make phone calls to your team and potential recruits on a regularly scheduled basis, and you may see changes in your communication style.

8 AND ABOVE You are an extrovert and have learned the art of communication. This skill most likely serves you well in sales and leadership. You consistently make an effort to talk to your people often and use active listening skills to really hear what they are saying. Through using encouraging words and empathy, you are a person others enjoy listening to and talking with. These skills will serve you well in your business.

COMMUNICATE OPENLY EXERCISE: Good communication doesn't just happen. It takes effort and practice. Take an hour out of each day to conduct your phone calls. Remember to be aware of your body language, voice and message. When on the phone, assume a relaxed smile — the receiver can hear it in your voice. Remember — listening is an active part of communication. Be present and attune when listening to the other person speak.

POWER HOUR RECORD

Use this to track your calls and record your results during your daily Power Hour. Use your communication skills during this time to be present and fully connect to others.

DATE	CONTACT NAME	CUSTOMER CALLS	HOSTESS CALLS

BOOKING CALLS	SPONSORING CALLS	RESULTS/FOLLOW UP NEEDED

STEP 6

Have Clear Priorities

When you become clear in your mind about what you want for yourself, you can begin setting priorities for achieving your goals. Your dream begins with a vision. It culminates by defining that vision in clear, concise and concrete terms. To make your dreams become a reality, you begin by setting goals and priorities that will lead you to your ultimate goal. Once you are completely clear about what you want, your passion and energy will show you the way. Your own set of expectations and drive will overcome any obstacles that get in your way, as long as you stay clear on your goals. Oftentimes, it is the overcoming the obstacles that helps you get there.

Write down your thoughts to get clear about your goals. You then begin prioritizing what you need to do to reach your destination. Think big — the end result is really limitless. You have a wealth of resources at your disposal within yourself. Take advantage of the many tools, resources and training available to help you. The more you can learn and reach out to others, the faster you will reach your goals. In direct sales it is important to Know the Way, Go the Way, and Show the Way, meaning know what you want, go the distance to achieve it, then show the opportunity to others.

"Lost time is never found again." Benjamin Franklin

- *I know where to concentrate my efforts for the highest return.*
  Like a ship traveling through a foreign sea, aim your sights on your destination, then set your sails and hold tight. Let nothing blow you off track. If you find yourself getting bogged down in a sea of paperwork or personnel problems, readjust your course and ride it out. If you allow yourself to get bogged down and lose focus on your goal, you may get off course. Don't get caught looking up at the end of the day still in your pajamas with projects half done! Make a list of priorities to help you systematically schedule your time to maximize your results. Realize that connecting with people and networking, while staying focused on booking, selling and recruiting, is how you will grow your business.

- *I start each day with a list of the top five things I want to accomplish.*
  Allow yourself 30 minutes of downtime to sit and think. Clarity can only come in a pool of calm waters — you can never see to the bottom of a rough sea. Empty your mind and allow the most important items you need to accomplish to surface. Write down the five most important items you wish to do, and you will be amazed at how you begin rearranging your time to focus on those priorities.

- *I work on (booking, selling, recruiting, training, promoting) my business 80% of the time and in it (paperwork, organizing filing) 20% of the time.*

  Remember the 80/20 rule and give 80% of your time to growing your business and building a team while focusing most of your time on your high performers, and 20% of your time on running the business – the necessary paperwork and organization. Sometimes it helps to schedule your activities in a planner. List phone calls you need to make and set weekly goals for booking, selling and recruiting. Tools like this will help you make a plan and stick to it.

- *I say "yes" only to those things that support my goals and vision.*

  Do you ever feel pulled in too many directions? Most women do. Between family, home, pets, husbands, friends, neighbors and volunteer work, it's a wonder we can get it all done. Many women are able to multi-task, but oftentimes we have trouble saying no. When life drives you instead of you being in the driver's seat, it's time to put on the brakes! When you begin asserting yourself with confidence, people take notice and will respect you for it. Do what you can to support your vision and let things that really aren't that important fall away.

- *I spend an hour each month with my top five influencers, individually building relationships.*

  As a leader, it is your job to help surround yourself with others and help them become successful. When you spend time supporting those who can help you reach your vision, everyone wins. The people who generate energy — not take it from you — are the ones you need to support the most. Foster relationships that create bottom line results. People with ideas and initiative are the ones who are unstoppable. Recognize those and arm them with resources and knowledge. When you can create an environment of trust, respect and positive rapport, there's nothing you can't accomplish. Working with others is the key to moving forward.

- *I schedule time each week for advancing in six areas of life, (Spirit, Health, Relationships, Mind, Business, Financial).*

  You've heard this over and over again—balance is important in life. This is often easier said than done. Analyze how much time you truly spend on your spirituality (relationship to God), your health (fitness and nutrition, your relationships (family, personal and work), your mind (reading, thinking, studying), business (booking, selling recruiting), and financial (accounting, taxes). Are you wasting some of your time and thoughts on things that really don't matter? Worry, negative thoughts, gossip, blaming or mischief are just a few things that get in the way of what's important. When you move into clear thinking and begin setting your priorities, you will find your wheel, and your life, begin to fill in and you become more complete and balanced.

- *I set aside uninterrupted time each day to work on ideas that expand my business.*
  Business leaders are beginning to see the value of meditation. Clearing your mind and doing activities like golf, tennis, quilting, or other recreational activities you enjoy actually enhance the way you think. Sometimes leaving your office and going to a coffee shop or park to sit and think can produce great results. Some people find a calm place to go every day, like a spa or bench in their yard, to sit and actively focus on ideas. A good idea will generate more than any amount of busy work ever could. Give yourself the space and time to think creatively.

- *I hire help or get assistance in areas that are not the best use of my time.*
  When you begin to see how productive you can be by setting clear priorities, you may realize some tasks can be delegated to others. Assign other family members chores like laundry, emptying the trash or cooking—it will be good for them and for you. When you begin making more money, you can hire help to do some of the cleaning, laundry, yard and cooking tasks that take so much of your time. Every woman needs help! Know you deserve it you will find that when you are willing to receive help from others, your needs will start to be met. There are many resources you can use. Allow yourself to hire help when you need it!

- *I take time to celebrate and appreciate my personal successes each week.*
  What is life about if not to feel gratitude and joy for all that you have accomplished? When you are happy about yourself and the great things you are able to do, that spills over into all the areas of you life. Happy people generate great relationships, so give yourself permission to enjoy your success! Take your husband out to dinner, treat yourself to a massage or buy a great new pair of shoes. You are worth it!

- *I make honesty a high priority in all circumstances.*
  One of the most destructive things we do as humans is to hide from our true selves. Rather than be honest and accepting of who we are, we engage in forms of denial, blame, irresponsible behavior, passive aggression, manipulation and negativity. We are often our own worst enemy! By serving others and finding joy in life, we can approach life with a more direct and positive attitude. It is possible to reprogram those old behaviors and begin living more honestly and happily. Be true to yourself, be truthful with others and live by the golden rule.

CHECK THE BOXES THAT APPLY TO YOU

Read the following statements and check what you feel are your strengths.
The boxes left blank may indicate areas you may need to work on.

❑ I know where to concentrate my efforts for the highest return.
❑ I start each day with a list of the top five things I want to accomplish.
❑ I work on (booking, selling, recruiting, training, promoting) my business 80%
   of the time and in it (paperwork, organizing filing) 20% of the time.
❑ I say "yes" only to those things that support my goals and vision.
❑ I spend an hour each month with my top five influencers, individually
   building relationships.
❑ I schedule time each week for advancing in six areas of life,
   (Spirit, Health, Relationships, Mind, Business, Financial).
❑ I set aside uninterrupted time each day to work on ideas that
   expand my business.
❑ I hire help or get assistance in areas that are not the best use of my time.
❑ I take time to celebrate and appreciate my personal successes each week..
❑ I make honesty a high priority in all circumstances.

___ Number of boxes checked (10 max)

SCORES

0-3 Take time to reevaluate your priorities. Talk your Director or find a mentor
or life coach to help if you have trouble prioritizing what is important. Take time
for self reflection and dedicate yourself to growing and become responsible for
your actions and your life. Know you are the most important person in your life
and deserve to live the life of your dreams.

4-7 You are doing a good job of setting priorities. If you feel bogged down in
certain areas of your life, make some adjustments and reevaluate your priorities.
Are you spending your time to further your goals? Write down what is important
and see if you are living to achieve what you want. Books you may want to read
are *Simple Abundance: A Daybook of Comfort and Joy* by Sarah Ban Breathnach and
The Artist's Way: A Spiritual Path to Higher Creativity by Julia Cameron.

8 AND ABOVE You have mastered living the life of your dreams! You have set
clear priorities that set you on the path to getting what you want out of life. Your
relationships, business, spirituality and wealth, mind and body are well balanced and
living a healthy and happy existence. Congratulations! You are achieving great things.

HAVE CLEAR PRIORITIES EXERCISE: By striving for balance, you will keep your priorities straight. This takes addressing every aspect of your life. Evaluate your life and starting in the middle, color in the pie according to how much time and energy you spend in each area. If you are like most people, your circle will end up looking like a spider web! This exercise is designed to help you look at the areas of your life that you may need to work on. As each section of the pie begins to fill up, you will find that the bumpy areas of your life begin to smooth out and like a full tire, things will begin rolling along more smoothly.

It takes a lot of work to tend to each area of your life, but you will find that by striving for balance, your lifestyle, relationships and health will steadily begin to improve. This will translate to your business. This "holistic" approach will enrich your life and lead to prosperity!

Take a colored pencil and beginning in the center, fill up how much time and energy you spend on each area in your own life.

STEP 7

Be a Change Leader

Change is difficult. The older we get, it seems, the more adverse to change we become. We get used to doing things like we've always done them. But if we can open ourselves up to positive change and embrace new ideas and shed old habits, change can be good after all! Our world is always changing and evolving. New technologies, ideas and methods are on the horizon and when approached with an open mind, can offer exciting possibilities in our lives and in our business.

With email, instant messaging, the Internet, phone and web conferencing, just to name a few, we have more tools and resources at our disposal than ever before. If you learn to use new technologies and keep up with trends in the marketplace, you can position yourself as one of the innovative individuals we call a Change Leader.

Change Leaders are always on the lookout for ways to improve how things are done. They are not afraid to embrace new ideas or change.

"Dreams pass into the reality of action. From the actions stems the dream again; and this interdependence produces the highest form of living." Anais Nin

- *I keep up with changes in the business in order to provide on-going training for my team.*
  Direct Sales is an exciting and dynamic industry, with new people and opportunities coming your way all the time. How can you stay afloat with all the changes? Education and knowledge are the answer. Keep yourself and your team trained at every opportunity.

- *I embrace change and help my team understand the need for and value of change.*
  Fear of rejection and fear of failure are two of the biggest obstacles to a willingness to change. Allow yourself and your team members to feel safe and open to change. Encourage them to try new strategies for sales success and to talk to people they've never talked to before. The most successful people in life are those who are willing to take risks and evolve!

- *I inform my team of changes in advance so they will have time to adapt.*
  Communication is key in motivating others to change behaviors. People need to know what is happening. Make sure they are clear and understand any changes that are taking place in your business or team. You will find they are much more

open if they know it is coming. No one likes unwelcome surprises. Make room for time and patience to allow others to adapt.

- *I explain the overall objectives of the change to my team – the reasons for it and how and when it will occur.*
Let your team members have a buy in – if they understand the why, when and how, they will be able to support the decision. Be aware of their feelings. When you inform them of changes in a compassionate and informative manner, they will respond more positively to new ways of doing things.

- *I encourage questions, comments and discussions revolving around changes.*
Reassurance and good listening skills go a long way when you are leading a team. Encourage questions through active listening and respectful feedback. Sometimes all they need is to be heard. Be open to discussing change in a mature and levelheaded manner and you will have better results.

- *I look for the opportunity in change and share such with my team.*
As a leader, constantly be on the look out for classes, motivation books and tapes and new avenues of revenue and opportunity for your team members. If you embrace change, so will they. Your enthusiasm and support will help. Look online. Google, Wikipedia and social networking media offer thousands of resources. Stay positive and focused when making changes and time will take care of the rest.

- *I express my confidence in my team's ability to "go with the flow" when change occurs.*
When people feel "out of control," they tend to tighten up on their control of their environment. Anyone who's ever had teenagers knows this feeling. Sometimes going with the flow and losing a tight grip on your "control issues" can do wonders. A healthy person is task-oriented and adaptable. Loosen up and trust that things will happen for the best. We can never be in the wrong place when it comes to learning and growing.

- *I transform and coach individuals to be leaders themselves.*
Empowering others to become the best they can be is the name of the game in Direct Sales. In the words of Zig Ziglar, "Make those around you successful and you will find your own success." Mentor those around you to be leaders, and you can effectively grow your team.

- *I look for and encourage others to share innovative approaches to business development.*
  Brainstorming sessions and spending time with your team will help you become an "idea-generating culture." Innovations in sales and customer service will help your business grow. Learn how to think in new directions.

- *I am continually learning new skills to improve professionally and personally.*
  The people who are on the lookout to constantly improve are the ones who get ahead. Self-improvement is the quest we are all on to raise ourselves to new heights and enrich and fulfill our lives.

CHECK THE BOXES THAT APPLY TO YOU

Read the following statements and check what you feel are your strengths. The boxes left blank may indicate areas you may need to work on.

- ❑ I keep up with changes in the business in order to provide on-going training for my team.
- ❑ I embrace change and help my team understand the need for and value of change.
- ❑ I inform my team of changes in advance so they will have time to adapt.
- ❑ I explain the overall objectives of the change to my team – the reasons for it and how and when it will occur.
- ❑ I encourage questions, comments and discussions revolving around changes.
- ❑ I look for the opportunity in change and share such with my team.
- ❑ I express my confidence in my team's ability to "go with the flow" when change occurs.
- ❑ I transform and coach individuals to be leaders themselves.
- ❑ I look for and encourage others to share innovative approaches to business development.
- ❑ I am continually learning new skills to improve professionally and personally.

___ Number of boxes checked (10 max)

SCORES

0-3 You've been living this way for many years and it works. But a little variety and spice never hurt anyone! Try opening yourself to new concepts and ideas and see what happens. You may want to find a job coach or sign up for a Continuing Education design class, computer class or public speaking course. Spend time online with a child or grandchild—they are marvels at embracing new technology. A little change may do you good!

4-7 You have made many positive changes in your life and it shows. Do you still find areas where you are resistant to change? Try approaching new ideas in a more positive light and be willing to explore new ways of doing things. Read John Maxwell's *Thinking for a Change* or Jeff Olson's *The Slight Edge*. They may inspire you to look at things in a whole new way.

8 AND ABOVE You are a Change Leader and realize that reinventing yourself is necessary in today's world. Women can be real chameleons when it comes to changing for the better or when it comes to improving the lives of those around them. Your openness to new ideas, willingness to learn and ability to strive to new heights has served you well!

BE A CHANGE LEADER EXERCISE: One way to change is through education. Here is a list of books you can read and tapes you can listen to open your mind to new ideas and new ways of doing things.

Think and Grow Rich, Napolean Hill

Build it Big, DSWA

Living the Exceptional Life, Jim Rohn

Superior Sales Management, Brian Tracy

Leadership 101, John Maxwell

The Success Principles, Jack Canfield

Think and Grow Rich, Napleon Hill

7 Habits of Highly Effective People, Stephen Covey

STEP 8

Be a Role Model

The best way to become a leader who others admire to is by living your life fully, responsibly and to the best of your ability. High-level leaders stay within their integrity and know they are truly responsible for their thoughts, feelings, actions and behaviors. They do not harbor a victim attitude or sit around waiting for life to happen. They embrace it fully and live in the present moment. It takes a great deal of self-love, humility, passion, vulnerability and graciousness to evolve into a role model. This takes a lot of emotional work and mindfulness. Sometimes old behaviors may need to be re-patterned for you to evolve into the natural leader you are. The power is within you, waiting to be tapped, but you must be willing to go the extra mile.

How you dress, how you behave, how to speak and how you interact with the world around you says a lot about how you feel about yourself. Others realize this and choose to follow those they respect and admire.

"Try not to become a man of success but rather try to become a man of value." Albert Einstein

- *I set a strong example by being a consistent seller and recruiter.*
  Role models can be counted on to have the discipline and fortitude it takes to make winning habitual. If you practice consistency in your life and business, you will see results, and others will take notice.

- *I project my self positively without exception.*
  Do you exude value and confidence? This is reflected in your actions and how you appear to others. Sometimes we need to take a hard look in the mirror and work on how we project ourselves to the world. This takes a great deal of self-reflection and courage and a willingness to change.

- *I reinvest part of my income in improving my abilities in speaking, leading, conducting meetings, selling, and motivating others.*
  Great leaders constantly work on self-improvement. This cannot be done alone. Resources abound to help you learn new skills and cultivate your abilities. Whether you would like to improve your public speaking, dress for success, learn new skills in technology or business, or cope with situations, invest part of the income you earn in yourself.

- *Besides learning new business skills, I also devote time to my personal development each quarter.*

Personal development takes work and a willingness to seek a higher level of awareness, consciousness, devotion and achievement. Reading books or listening to tapes by great leaders and philosophers is one way to gain insight. Finding a life coach or mentor may be helpful as well. Our spiritual growth is as important and will only add to our relationships, business dealings and financial growth.

- *I make improving my professional image a priority.*
  Taking care to dress, groom and take care of yourself is one way to show others that we feel positive and in tune with ourselves. If you need help in this area, reach out to a personal fitness trainer, wardrobe Consultant, makeup Consultant or hair stylist. No need to spend too much or go overboard, but making an effort to look and feel your best allows you to put your best foot forward, while wearing great shoes, of course!

- *I have at least two daily personal practices that are restorative for me (meditation, relaxation exercises, yoga/pilates, healthy eating, reading, walking, etc.).*
  To keep your life in balance, take time out for yourself. Learning how to quiet the mind takes a surprising amount of self-discipline. If you can get in the habit of meditation, exercise and mindfulness, you will find you have more self-control, harmony and balance in your life.

- *I model how to deal with mistakes by being accountable for my own.*
  Leaders do not play the blame game. Nor do they skirt the truth or manipulate to force a situation in their favor. They accept the consequences of their actions and vocalize an apology if necessary, then move on to rectify the situation. They are accountable for their decisions and learn from their mistakes.

- *I practice living in the present moment, letting go of the past and not fearing the future.*
  This is easier said than done—we spend much of our mental state dwelling the past or worrying about the future. The past is done. The future an illusion. The only moment we have is right now. We must respond to situations, not react. Read Barbara Johnson's book, "Stick a geranium in your hat and be happy."

- *I make a list of at least five things for which I am grateful everyday.*
  When you pay your water and electric bill, are you angry or grateful? Try being glad you have fresh running water and the ability to turn on lights and AC to make your environment pleasant. Are you grateful for the sunset, the wonderful earth and its inhabitants? Gratitude is an attitude and one we should all be better at practicing.

- *I know that thoughts create reality and I quickly return to positive thoughts when negative ones surface.*

  It is so easy to allow ourselves to get sucked into self-pity, grief, denial, addictions. Blaming and self-critical thoughts. Many of these feelings are fear-based and not really true at all! Do not deny your feelings, but try to look at things in a more positive and realistic light. Your thoughts really do control your reality. In the words of Dale Carnegie, "It is the way we react to circumstances that determines our feelings. "

CHECK THE BOXES THAT APPLY TO YOU

Read the following statements and check what you feel are your strengths. The boxes left blank may indicate areas you may need to work on.

❑ I set a strong example by being a consistent seller and recruiter.

❑ I project my self positively without exception.

❑ I reinvest part of my income in improving my abilities in speaking, leading, conducting meetings, selling, and motivating others.

❑ Besides learning new business skills, I also devote time to my personal development each quarter.

❑ I make improving my professional image a priority.

❑ I have at least 2 daily personal practices that are restorative for me (meditation, relaxation exercises, yoga, healthy eating, reading, walking, etc.).

❑ I model how to deal with mistakes by being accountable for my own.

❑ I practice living in the present moment, letting go of the past and not fearing the future.

❑ I make a list of at least five things for which I am grateful everyday.

❑ I know that thoughts create reality and I quickly return to positive thoughts when negative ones surface.

___ Number of boxes checked (10 max)

SCORES

0-3 You have the ability to improve and make steps toward becoming someone others respect and admire. You can work on your balance and self-esteem by taking positive steps in your everyday life. As you begin your journey to a higher sense of gratitude, fulfillment and embracing life, others will be amazed at the changes they see within you.

4-7 As an up and coming leader you show many of the attributes and attitudes it takes to be a role model to others. Continue working on your personal growth, character and enhancing your qualities to be the best you can be.

8 AND ABOVE You are a natural leader and role model to others. It takes a great deal of maturity and fairness to be a person in your position and you must take great care not to take advantage of your status. Others look to you for inspiration and motivation. You are engendered with leading others and have an obligation to act responsibly and trustworthy in all situations.

BE A ROLE MODEL EXERCISE: As you think about becoming a successful role model, the answer is to hold lots of parties/shows. Here are some booking word choices to make it easier for you to schedule shows. Your team is watching and listening to you, so what you say will influence how they approach others. Never walk alone. Always take a new consultant with you. You will teach him or her to demonstrate product, close the sale and write up orders. Plus, you receive better energy while showing someone else how!

- *"If you were to host a party, who would you invite?"*
- *"If you were to host a party, what gift would you like to receive?"*
- *"If you were to host a party show, when would be the best time for you and your friends – afternoon or evening?"*
- *"If you were to host a party, where would be the best place for you and your friends – at the office or at your home?"*
- *"I would love for you to be one of my Hostess!"*
- *"A Double Hostess Show would be great for you and a friend!"*
- *"Let me tell you why this month is the very best time to host a party."*
- *"I'm calling back all of my favorite Hostesses because there's a fantastic new product we introduced and I wanted you to be one of the first to see!"*
- *"Place party cards on the table. When you choose one you will receive this extra gift tonight."*
- *"The post it notes on the table have available dates. When you book one tonight you will receive this extra gift . . ."*

STEP 9

....

Value People

People are what make the world go around. Do you value people? Do you value yourself? Sometimes as humans we forget the most essential part of life are the people in it. We get so wrapped up in our day-to-day stress, finances, material things, worries and struggles, we sometimes forget that people are our most wonderful resource and relationships our most cherished possession.

Were you valued as a child? Do you make those around you feel as though they are of value and appreciated? It takes a special person to make others feel as though they are esteemed and worthwhile.

"In order to be irreplaceable one must always be different." Coco Chanel

- *I treat each member of my team with respect, dignity and kindness.*
  All people deserve to be treated well. The Golden Rule holds true in all your dealings with others.

- *I take the initiative to mentor an inexperienced team member.*
  People are often hesitant to ask for help, even when the need it the most. Try to take a pro-active approach to get others involved and impart your valuable knowledge and experience to others.

- *I welcome ideas from others and let them know.*
  If you come from an open-minded and non-judgmental; mind set, others will feel more compelled to share their ideas with you. Business is built on ideas. Allow your team members and others the latitude to brainstorm, converse and think up new ideas.

- *I maintain a profile of each personal recruit detailing desires, goals, achievements and personal information.*
  People enjoy sharing this information with you. Everyone has a unique set of beliefs and passions. By tapping into what motivates them, you can get to know them better and their talents can serve you well.

- *I attribute part of my success as a leader to helping others develop.*
  People like being with others who challenge them. Are you a person who raises the bar just by striving to be good at what you do? Invest your time and energy into others to help them grow and you will reap rewards ten-fold.

- *I know exactly what makes each key team member feel appreciated and I honor her preference.*
  Know what makes team members tick and show them how much you **CARE**. (**C**ommunication, **A**ppreciating, **R**ecognition and **E**ncouragement.)

- *I make myself available to team members who seek my counsel.*
  Are you someone whom others can confide? Do they feel safe in telling you their secrets or asking for your advice? If others trust you and respect your opinion you can become a wonderful source of wisdom for them.

- *I frequently ask team members what they need from me in order to reach their full potential.*
  When people's needs are being met, they feel less frustrated and more supported to be able to function at their highest level. Have you done your due diligence to ensure your team has the knowledge, tools and support they need to succeed?

- *I know the strengths and talents of each team member and emphasize these.*
  Sarah may be great at accounting. Betsy might enjoy cold calling on the phone. If you can tap into peoples' strengths and work synergistically as a team, you can grow a strong organization.

- *I recognize each team member for her contribution and creativity.*
  Do your team members know how you feel? So often we neglect telling others how we feel. A little encouragement goes a long way.

CHECK THE BOXES THAT APPLY TO YOU

Read the following statements and check what you feel are your strengths.
The boxes left blank may indicate areas you may need to work on.

- ❏ I treat each member of my team with the same respect, dignity and kindness.
- ❏ I take the initiative to mentor an inexperienced team member.
- ❏ I welcome ideas from others and let them know.
- ❏ I maintain a profile of each personal recruit detailing desires, goals, achievements and personal information.
- ❏ I attribute part of my success as a leader to helping others develop.
- ❏ I know exactly what makes key team members feel appreciated and I honor their preference.
- ❏ I make myself available to team members who seek my counsel.
- ❏ I frequently ask team members what they need from me in order to reach their full potential.
- ❏ I know the strengths and talents of each team member and emphasize these.
- ❏ I recognize each team member for her contribution and creativity.

___ Number of boxes checked (10 max)

SCORES

0-3 We learn by how we are treated as children. Sometimes when we begin looking we can see places where old patterns of behaviors must be altered to bring new joy into our present-day relationships. This takes emotional work. Transitioning from a self-centered perspective into a more giving individual can improve your relationships in all areas of your life.

4-7 You have made great strides in treating others how you would like to be treated. It takes a great deal of consideration and graciousness to look at the world through the eyes of others to determine how they may be thinking and feeling.

8 AND ABOVE You have done a lot of practice working with others and helping them to succeed. It is a sign of maturity and much personal growth to aspire to true leadership. You have demonstrated heightened interpersonal skills and know how to build strong teams.

VALUE PEOPLE EXERCISE: Show people you value them by keeping up with their personal information. When you recognize them by remembering their birthdays, children's names and other personal details, it lets them know they are important. Send small gifts and cards and stay in touch to let them know you care (remember **EMA** — **E**ncourage, **M**otivate and **A**ppreciate!) It is important to make notes about your customers and everyone on your team. To do this, use a database or tickler file to keep track of your networking contracts. For example:

NAME	EMAIL	PHONE	BIRTHDAY	KIDS NAMES	NOTES

Take a test to determine your strengths. Go to *www.DSLC.com*. Learn your strengths and focus on them!

- Use charms, pins or ribbons for consultants.
- Send birthday cards to your consultants and customers.
- Use a 12 month tickler file or an excel spreadsheet to keep track.

STEP 10

Accept Responsibility

A high level individual is responsible in their actions in every area of their life. This is a process that takes time to develop and cultivate and one that every human being should aspire. A heightened prosperity comes to those who are responsible. When you are building a team it is up to you and no one else. As a business owner, you have no one telling you what to do, where to be, and where to go. You are the master of your universe and know you have what it takes to design your life. While you will make plenty of mistakes along the way, as a responsible person you will acknowledge them and learn from them.

"The price of greatness is responsibility." Winston Churchill

- *I am responsible for providing the leadership, tools and training that my team needs.*
  You will never be an effective team leader unless you provide the proper training and tools to your team. They are looking to you for encouragement, help and advice. You are key to their success and it is your obligation and responsibility to guide your team to greatness.

- *I understand that I am responsible for the overall performance of the team, NOT for each person's individual success.*
  Enabling is not the same as supporting. Be careful not to put all your energy into the non-productive members or your team and neglect the 20 percent who are high-performing. It is your mission to get everyone operating on all cylinders and to do this takes the efforts of everyone. Let your team members know they are responsible for their own success as a contributing part of the team.

- *I am responsible for setting the attitude of the team -- one of mutual respect and service.*
  Don't let your team members fall into the trap of self-destructive behaviors. It is your job to let them know there is no room for cattiness, selfishness, one-upmanship or ostracizing other team members. You set the tone as respectful and positive and others will follow suit.

- *I take responsibility for mistakes I make and see them as growth opportunities.*
  Blaming others for your mistakes or shortcomings is no way to live your life. Don't try to hide your faux pas, but be honest and up front and know you will do better in the future.

- *I am responsible for building a strong relationship with team members.*
Create opportunities for your team members to bond. Invite your team to your house for a brunch or brain storming session. Rent out a trade booth or show to advertise your business together. Unifying the individuals in a team effort makes a strong and productive environment.

- *I am responsible for my own personal sales and recruiting results and for setting the example for my team.*
When you attain the level for having a team it is time to get busy — not rest on your laurels. More than ever you must roll up your sleeves and get to work. Your team members are watching your queue and will follow your example.

- *I am responsible for maintaining high integrity and modeling this for my team.*
Whenever you are out of integrity, it will show up in every aspect of your life. Whenever you tell a white lie, cover up a mistake, gossip behind someone's back, try to get something for nothing, use others or become involved mischievous or manipulative behavior, you are out of integrity. You know it and others will know it. True character is how you behave when no one is looking.

- *I am responsible for creating an environment conducive to trusting and sharing.*
Set the pillars of your team straight in the beginning and you will have a strong foundation that will last. Trust is earned and easily broken, and hard to repair. Be aware of everyone's feelings and approach problems in a direct and honest way. Be open to sharing and you can foster an attitude of trust.

- *I am responsible for developing strong leaders under me.*
Leaders are not born; they are made. It is your job to cultivate and teach people to evolve into leaders. This takes patience, understanding, accountability and time.

- *I study my retention data monthly and get input on what I can do to improve.*
Numbers speak volumes. When you are not seeing results, don't keep doing the same thing. It's your job to make it work. You are making important steps in looking to see where your deficiencies and strengths lie. Keep working on yourself and improving and you will get the results you desire.

CHECK THE BOXES THAT APPLY TO YOU

Read the following statements and check what you feel are your strengths. The boxes left blank may indicate areas you may need to work on.

❑ I am responsible for providing the leadership, tools and training that my team needs.

❑ I understand that I am responsible for the overall performance of the team, NOT for each person's individual success.

❑ I am responsible for setting the attitude of the team -- one of mutual respect and service.

❑ I take responsibility for mistakes I make and see them as growth opportunities.

❑ I am responsible for building a strong relationship with team members.

❑ I am responsible for my own personal sales and recruiting results and for setting the example for my team.

❑ I am responsible for maintaining high integrity and modeling this for my team.

❑ I am responsible for creating an environment conducive to trusting and sharing.

❑ I am responsible for developing strong leaders under me.

❑ I study my retention data monthly and get input on what I can do to improve.

___ Number of boxes checked (10 max)

SCORES

0-3 You are beginning to see some areas you can work on to become more responsible. That's great and is a huge part of growing up. You are beginning to see that you are solely responsible for your feelings, behaviors and attitudes. Old patterns die hard, but you are willing to work on change. As you become more responsible, you will soon see the drama and tension in your life evaporating and making room for more harmony and balance.

4-7 You are well on you way to the path of responsible behavior. Responsibility means you have the *Ability to Respond* to every situation in a pragmatic, task-oriented and healthy way. When you stay true to your morals and ethics, you open yourself up to all the abundance and success that is meant to be yours.

8 AND ABOVE You are a high-level leader who has taken the steps necessary to being a responsible person who is independent and capable. You are cognizant of staying within your integrity and because of this, have fostered an attitude of trust, mutual respect and synergy with your team. You realize your work has just begun and you have what it takes to have the ultimate life.

ACCEPT RESPONSIBILITY EXERCISE: Pay attention to your retention data. Think of ways to improve. Let your prospects know you have confidence in their abilities and you will be there to help them achieve success.

SPONSORING - OVERCOMING OBJECTIONS

I don't have enough time.
Your response: I can appreciate that because I choose to be a busy person too. That's why I selected you – busy people seem to get the most done. If I could show you how to turn 4 – 5 hours a week into $500 profit, could you find the 4 - 5 hours in a week?

I can't sell.
Actually, the product sells itself! We aren't looking for "sales" people, we want people like you to share with friends and family.

I'm already working a full time job.
Great! You will have a lot of contacts for your business. A lot of people work their business part time for extra income.

I love my job.
Great! Could you use some extra money? How do you know you won't like this career as well? You owe it to yourself to at least hear all the facts.

I don't have the money.
Great! That is the best reason of all for joining.

My children are too small.
Perfect! You will love the flexibility this career offers. You schedule the hours you want to work.

I can't be like you.
I wouldn't want you to be. I want you to be the best YOU can be.

I have never sold anything.
No problem. If I could teach you to do what I do, do you think you could learn? And, we have ongoing training available.

I need to think about it.
- What exactly do you need to think about? (find out her why)
- Let me ask you this. What is the one thing stopping you from getting a kit and making money next week?

The time just isn't right for me now.
I know how you feel, I felt the same way, what I found is – there's never a perfect time. The time to do anything will never be perfect, but we weigh the pros and cons and make our decision anyway.

I don't want to impose on my friends.
I can understand how you may feel that way, but let me ask you, do you like our product? You'll be providing your friends and acquaintances with a valuable service and they will appreciate it. Let's make a list of people you know who might enjoy it.

I'm too shy.
I know how you feel, I felt the same way, what I found is … once I completed my training, I was a lot more comfortable. And in the beginning, we are with our friends and family to "practice" on.

I don't think I can be up in front of people.
Feel – felt – found….. My friends made it easier to start with.

My husband doesn't want me to work:
I think it's great that your husband is showing an interest in your future. But how can he make a decision for you without knowing all the facts? I'm sure when he hears the advantages of our opportunity, he will be completely behind you.

I'm a single mom, I need the security of a "real" job.
That's exactly why I thought of you. In this career, your finances are not based on someone else's opinion of your "value" but on your ability to make as much as you want. You can determine your own paycheck, raise and security.

I don't know anyone.
Great! This will give you the opportunity to meet so many people. All you need is one person that is how it starts. Do you know three people? We can build a great list from that.

I need to think about it.
Wonderful, I will follow up with you on _____ to see if you have any further questions.

TAKE THE QUIZZES

It all starts with a vision, and requires becoming a responsible leader. Have your team members check the boxes on the following statements that they feel are their strengths. The boxes left blank may indicate areas to work on.

A. TRUST/INTEGRITY

❑ I always operate from a base of integrity (honesty), even in difficult situations.

❑ I under promise and over deliver.

❑ I work for a company that has high standards and integrity.

❑ I can be trusted to maintain confidences.

❑ I tell the truth 100% of the time.

❑ I keep my team informed about changes in the business.

❑ I honor my commitments always.

❑ I return all phone calls and answer emails the same day.

❑ I focus on building long-term relationships with my team.

❑ I teach my team to demonstrate excellent standards of professionalism.

___ Number of boxes checked (10 max)

B. INSPIRED VISION

❑ I have a clear vision of where I am taking my business and what it feels like to be living this vision.

❑ I have communicated my vision to my team.

❑ I replace negative beliefs, attitudes or fears that block my vision with positive thoughts, words and actions.

❑ I know my core values and can easily relate these values to my vision.

❑ I continually develop skills or acquire knowledge to support reaching my vision.

❑ I know why I am in this business and can clearly articulate it in one sentence.

❑ I understand that I must be accepted as a leader first, before my teams can buy-in to my vision.

- ❑ As a visionary leader I help my team move beyond a focus on minor satisfactions to a quest for self-fulfillment.
- ❑ I know the dreams and visions of my team and seek to help them get what they want.
- ❑ I hold periodic brainstorming sessions with an innovative core group to spark new ideas or approaches for achieving our visions.

___ Number of boxes checked (10 max)

C. UNDERSTANDING BASICS OF YOUR BUSINESS

- ❑ I understand that contact is an essential element in leadership.
- ❑ I challenge team members and hold them accountable for their commitments.
- ❑ I celebrate the successes of each team member no matter how small.
- ❑ I personally recognize team members accomplishments at meetings, by email, mail or phone.
- ❑ I understand the desires of my team and how to best motivate them.
- ❑ I replicate what I am doing by training new sales managers in my team.
- ❑ I understand part of my leadership role is to coach others to take responsibility.
- ❑ I resist the urge to tell others what to do and instead, use open-ended questions to guide them to their own solutions.
- ❑ I have identified the high-performing 20% of my team so that I can coach and encourage them with weekly contact.
- ❑ I **CARE** enough about each team member to let them know through: **C**ommunication, **A**ppreciation, **R**ecognition, and **E**ncouragement.

___ Number of boxes checked (10 max)

D. BE AN ENERGY GENERATOR

- ❑ I love what I do and it shows.
- ❑ I am passionate about my business, my team and serving others.
- ❑ I make a conscious choice to be positive about my business and to reflect such.
- ❑ I know what restores my energy and I schedule time for such activities each week.
- ❑ I start each morning enthusiastic about what's ahead.
- ❑ I know that my attitude, as a leader, is picked up more quickly by my team than my actions.
- ❑ I quickly deal with anything that depletes my energy (i.e.- clutter, unanswered mail, piles of papers or forms, broken equipment, etc).
- ❑ My team is motivated, producing, and excited about their success.
- ❑ I know that it's not circumstances that affect my energy, that instead, it is my reaction to these circumstances.
- ❑ If problems arise within the team, I address them immediately, rather than put it off.

___ Number of boxes checked (10 max)

E. COMMUNICATE OPENLY

❑ I have regularly scheduled times to communicate with my team.

❑ I understand the four behavioral styles and know how to effectively communicate with each.

❑ I use a supportive communication style, seeking to make team members feel good about themselves.

❑ I continually seek new ways to improve my communication skills.

❑ I frequently interact with team members at all levels.

❑ I practice effective listening giving others opportunity to share their input.

❑ I am truthful and consistent in my communications, sharing the information with each person.

❑ I deliver unpleasant news in person, when possible, and in a calm, non-judgmental manner.

❑ I understand that the purpose of communication is not just to convey information, but also to change behavior by persuading people to take action.

❑ I listen to learn, to grow, to encourage and to convey that I care.

___ Number of boxes checked (10 max)

F. HAVE CLEAR PRIORITIES

❑ I know where to concentrate my efforts for the highest return.

❑ I start each day with a list of the top five things I want to accomplish.

❑ I work on, (servicing, selling, recruiting, promoting, training), my business 80% of the time and in it (paperwork, organizing, filing), 20%.

❑ I say yes only to those things that support my goals and vision.

❑ I spend an hour per month with my top five influencers, individually, building relationships.

❑ I schedule time each week for advancing in six life areas, (Spirit, Health, Relationships, Mind, Business, Financial).

❑ I set aside uninterrupted time each day to work on ideas that expand my business.

❑ I hire help or get assistance in areas that are not the best use of my time.

❑ I take time to celebrate and appreciate my personal successes each week.

❑ I make honesty a high priority in all circumstances.

___ Number of boxes checked (10 max)

G. BE A CHANGE LEADER

❑ I keep up with changes in the business in order to provide on-going training to my team.

❑ I embrace change and help my team understand the need for and value of change.

❑ I inform my team of changes in advance so they will have time to adapt.

❑ I explain the overall objectives of the change to my team the reasons for it and how and when it will occur.

❑ I encourage questions, comments and discussion revolving around changes.

❑ I look for the opportunity in change and share such with my team.

❑ I express my confidence in my team's ability to go with the flow when change occurs.

❑ I transform and coach individuals to be leaders themselves.

❑ I look for, and encourage others to share, innovative approaches to business development.

❑ I am continually learning new skills to improve professionally and personally.

___ Number of boxes checked (10 max)

H. BE A ROLE MODEL

❏ I set a strong example by being a consistent seller and recruiter.

❏ I project my self positively without exception.

❏ I reinvest part of my income in improving my abilities in speaking, leading, conducting meetings, selling, and motivating others.

❏ Besides learning new business skills, I also devote time to my personal development each quarter.

❏ I make improving my professional image a priority.

❏ I have at least two daily personal practices that are restorative for me (meditation, relaxation exercises, yoga, healthy eating, reading, walking, etc.).

❏ I model how to deal with mistakes by being accountable for my own.

❏ I practice living in the present moment, letting go of the past and not fearing the future.

❏ I make a list of at least five things for which I am grateful everyday.

❏ I know that thoughts create reality and I quickly return to positive thoughts when negative ones surface.

___ Number of boxes checked (10 max)

I. VALUE PEOPLE

❏ I treat each member of my team with the same respect, dignity and kindness.

❏ I take the initiative to mentor an inexperienced team member.

❏ I welcome ideas from others and let them know.

❏ I maintain a profile of each personal recruit detailing desires, goals, achievements and personal information.

❏ I attribute part of my success as a leader to helping others develop.

❏ I know exactly what makes key team members feel appreciated and I honor their preference.

❏ I make myself available to team members who seek my counsel.

- ❑ I frequently ask team members what they need from me in order to reach their full potential.
- ❑ I know the strengths and talents of each team member and emphasize these.
- ❑ I recognize each team member for her contribution and creativity.
- ___ Number of boxes checked (10 max)

J. ACCEPT RESPONSIBILITY

- ❑ I am responsible for providing the leadership, tools and training that my team needs.
- ❑ I understand that I am responsible for the overall performance of the team,
- ❑ NOT for each person's individual success.
- ❑ I am responsible for setting the attitude of the team -- one of mutual respect and service.
- ❑ I take responsibility for mistakes I make and see them as growth opportunities.
- ❑ I am responsible for building a strong relationship with team members.
- ❑ I am responsible for my own personal sales and recruiting results and for setting the example for my team.
- ❑ I am responsible for maintaining high integrity and modeling this for my team.
- ❑ I am responsible for creating an environment conducive to trusting and sharing.
- ❑ I am responsible for developing strong leaders under me.
- ❑ I study my retention data monthly and get input on what I can do to improve.
- ___ Number of boxes checked (10 max)

DIRECT SELLING LEADERSHIP SUCCESS PROGRAM PROGRESS

TODAY	2ND QUARTER	3RD QUARTER	4TH QUARTER
A. TRUST/INTEGRITY Score:	A. Score:	A. Score:	A. Score:
B. INSPIRED VISION Score:	B. Score:	B. Score:	B. Score:
C. UNDERSTANDING BASICS OF YOUR BUSINESS Score:	C. Score:	C. Score:	C. Score:
D. BE AN ENERGY GENERATOR Score:	D. Score:	D. Score:	D. Score:
E. COMMUNICATE OPENLY Score:	E. Score:	E. Score:	E. Score:
F. CLEAR PRIORITIES Score:	F. Score:	F. Score:	F. Score:
G. BE A CHANGE LEADER Score:	G. Score:	G. Score:	G. Score:
H. BE A ROLE MODEL Score:	H. Score:	H. Score:	H. Score:
I. VALUE PEOPLE Score:	I. Score:	I. Score:	I. Score:
J. ACCEPT RESPONSIBILITY Score:	J. Score:	J. Score:	J. Score:

Take the individual totals by section from the previous sheets and fill in the columns from the bottom up. This is a great visual tool to see where you are in your leadership development.

You can easily see areas where you excel and areas that may still need attention. Update the chart quarterly as you progress to achieve a score of 10 in all categories!

THE FIRST STEP

"Life is a series of steps. Things are done gradually. Once in a while there is a giant step, but most of the time we are taking small, seemingly insignificant steps on the stairway of life."
Ralph Ransom

You have taken your first step toward success. Hopefully these exercises allowed you to reflect on your strengths and weakness so you can begin taking steps in the right direction. These exercises should tell you where you want to focus and give you some tips for how to begin. Start using tools like the Calendar, FRANK List, Power Hour and tickler file to help you.

It is time to take action. You may not know exactly where you might end up, but with courage and perseverance, you will begin the journey toward the life of your dreams. Proverbs 29:18 say "Where there is not vision the people will perish." Crystallize your dreams and you will find doors beginning to open for you. If you experience fear, that's OK. This is signaling that you are undergoing change and this is how we grow. FEAR is False Evidence Appearing Real and is easily overcome through a positive mindset and action.

When I first began my career in direct sales, I started out so I could afford to hire a housekeeper. Then I wanted some extra income to buy my husband and children gifts that would enrich their lives. Soon, I began saving up for a family vacation to Disney Land. Each of my dreams were realized, but the truly wonderful part was how I began growing as a person. At first I was afraid to speak to strangers, then I began making more friends than ever. I was once terrified of public speaking, and now am asked regularly to speak in front of large audiences. I am grateful everyday for the fantastic journey my career has taken me and I want to share this joy and freedom with other women.

I leave you with a special gift. Go to **www.DSLC.com** for an additional tip that will help jump-start your business. Log on by typing your personal information. On this site, you will find additional resources, training, business tools, incentive gifts and links to other sites that will open up doors to new ways of thinking.

Now, take the first step toward your success!